Early one bright spring morning, Peter went out into the garden. His friend the bird was sitting in a tree on the other side of the fence.

"Good morning, Peter," trilled the bird.

"Good morning," Peter answered. "I'm coming out into the meadow."

"All right," said the bird, and Peter opened the garden gate all by himself.

Sergey S. Prokofiev's

PETER AND THE WOLF

illustrated by Kōzō Shimizu

photographed by Yasuji Yajima

retold by Ann King Herring

Fantasia Pictorial
Stories from Famous Music

Soon a duck came waddling up to the gate. She was delighted when she found it open, because now she, too, could go out into the meadow, and take a morning swim on the pond.

When the little bird saw the duck paddling in the water, he flew down on to the grass, fluffed out his feathers importantly and started to tease her.

"You're a funny sort of a bird, aren't you?" he said to the duck. "Just look at you! You can't even fly."

But the duck only laughed at him. "Who are you to talk?" she quacked. "You call yourself a bird, but just look at you! You can't even swim."

They quarrelled and quarrelled, but neither one would give in. Just then, Peter noticed something. It was a cat, creeping ever so quietly through the grass.

"I'll catch that bird for my breakfast,
before he even knows it," thought the
cat.

"Look out!" shouted Peter. The bird
flew straight up into the tree. The duck
quacked loudly, from a safe distance
right in the middle of the pond.

Just then, Peter's grandfather came out. He was very, very angry.

"How many times have I told you not to go into the meadow?" he scolded. "It is more dangerous than you can imagine. Tell me now, just what would you do if a wolf came out of the forest?"

Needless to say, Peter was not at all perturbed. He would not be afraid of a dozen wolves.

But Grandfather had made up his mind.
He took Peter's hand, led him back inside
the gate . . . and locked it firmly after them.
    Just as soon as the gate was locked,
Grandpapa's fears came true.

An enormous wolf came bounding out of the forest. The quick-thinking cat clambered up into the tree. The duck quacked louder than ever. She was so frightened that she foolishly jumped out of the water and tried to run.

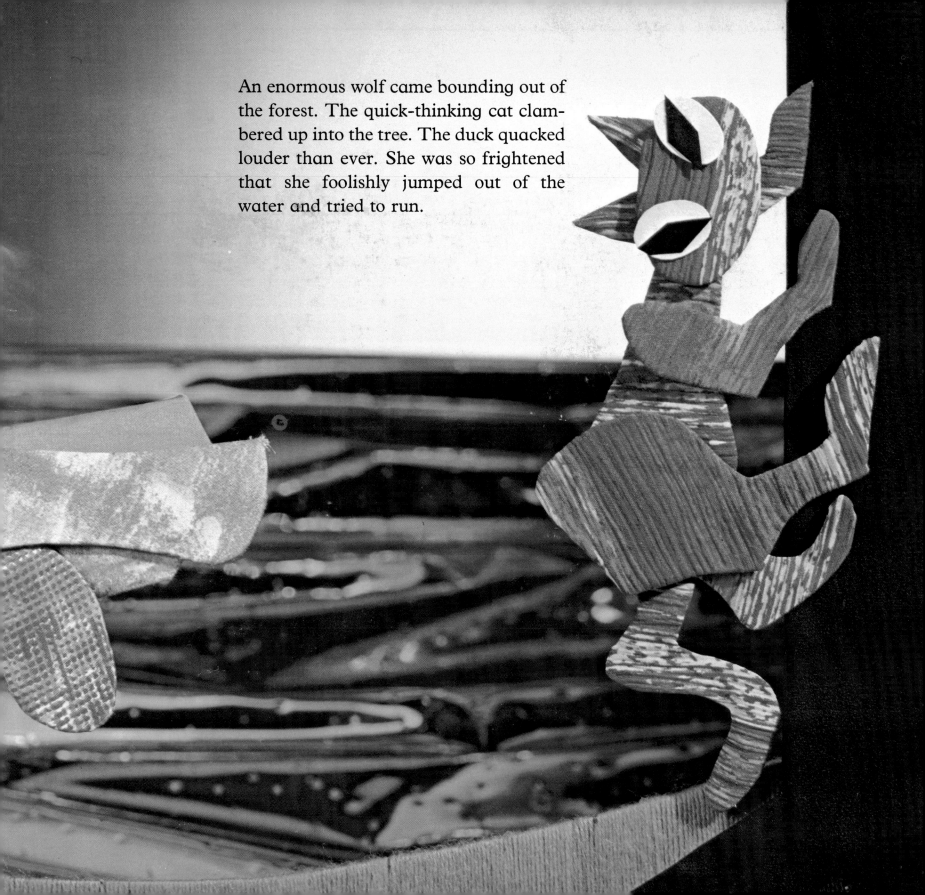

But her legs were far too short. No matter how hard she tried, she could only waddle, and there was no chance of escape.

Closer came the wolf and closer. Snap! He caught her, and gulp! In one bite, he swallowed her whole.

So that was that for the duck. And as for the others, you can imagine how things were. The cat was standing on a branch at one side of the tree, while the bird was perched on a branch at the other side—as far away as possible from the cat.

On the ground below, the wolf stalked around and around, staring greedily up at them both.

All this time, Peter had been standing behind the gate watching everything that was happening. Soon, he ran into the house. When he came out again, he was carrying a strong rope. Then he climbed on to the garden fence and swung himself into the tree.

"Fly down, now, and keep circling around the wolf's head, just as fast as you can," Peter said to the bird. "But be careful not to let him catch you!"

Snap! Snap! went the wolf. But the clever bird was too quick for him.

Peter made a noose in the end of the rope. Carefully, quickly, he let it down and . . .

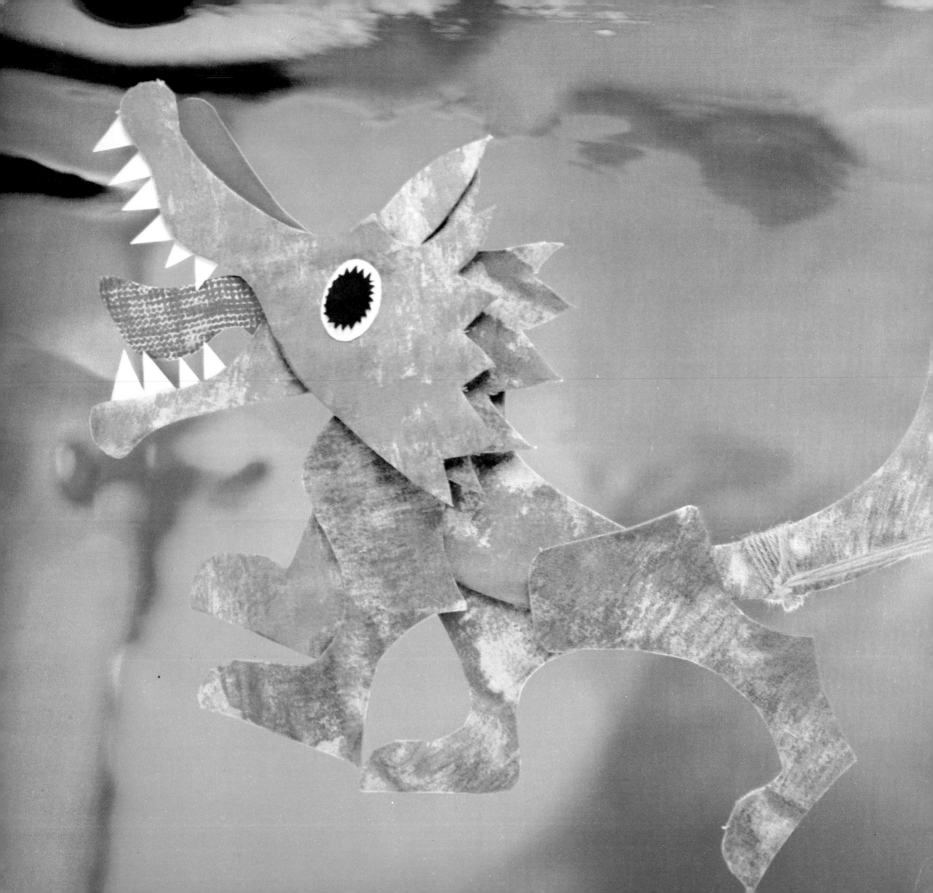

with a jerk, he caught the wolf by the tail. How
surprised that wolf was! He jumped up and
down, and this way and that way, trying to free
himself. But Peter had already tied the other
end of the rope to the tree, and the more fiercely
the wolf struggled, the tighter the knot became.

At that moment, Peter heard a noise of shooting. Some hunters came out of the forest, hot on the wolf's trail.

"Don't shoot!" cried Peter. "Look! We have caught the wolf already, the bird and I. Please help us take him to the zoo."

Then they all opened their eyes wide with surprise. From somewhere deep inside the wolf, they heard a steady quacking. It was the duck . . . for, in his haste, the wolf had gulped her down alive.

And so the triumphant procession set off. Peter, of course, marched at the head. After him strode the hunters with the captured wolf.

The little bird perched on Peter's hat and warbled cheerily. "Just see what Peter and I have done!" he sang.

Last of all walked Grandpapa and the cat. "These things are all very well, but . . ." muttered Grandpapa, shaking his head grumpily, "what if Peter had NOT caught the wolf? Hm? What then?"